WestBow Press books may be ordered through booksellers or by contacting:

WestBow Press
A Division of Thomas Nelson & Zondervan
1663 Liberty Drive
Bloomington, IN 47403
www.westbowpress.com
1 (866) 928-1240

ISBN: 978-1-4908-4339-1 (sc)
ISBN: 978-1-4908-4340-7 (e)

Library of Congress Control Number: 2014911827

Printed in the United States of America.

WestBow Press rev. date: 11/6/2014

WESTBOW
PRESS
A DIVISION OF THOMAS NELSON
& ZONDERVAN

To Kate, your love and friendship breathes life into me everyday.
To Tom, a wonderful guide and friend on this journey
and Ursula, for your patience and beautifully inspired illustrations.

This book belongs
to Princess:

Princess Ellie

Writer – Stuart Macklin

Editor – Tom Frye

Illustrator – Ursula Andrejczuk

Once upon a time, there was a beautiful princess named Ellieanne. Of course, she was called this by her mother and father, the queen and king, but her good friends simply called her Ellie.

Ellie's friends often said, "Our dear, sweet Princess Ellie has a magical light inside of her which brightens up our lives!"

Princess Ellie's close circle of friends claimed
she was the most beautiful girl in the world.
They found her to be sweet and nice, and
whenever she entered a room, every one of her
friends felt happier, and she caused them to
smile and then to giggle.

In her father's forest kingdom, when
Ellie skips through the forest, she lights
up with shimmering colours, which
causes even creatures like the squirrels,
the foxes, the bears and deer to gaze in
wonder as she crosses their paths.

But one day as Princess Ellie skipped through the forest, she met an evil frog sitting on a lily pad. Raspyputin was his name, for his voice was harsh and raspy, as if his words scraped across sandpaper whenever he spoke.

"Why are you skipping so happily?" Raspy asked. "I would think you would have plenty to worry about, my dear."

Princess Ellie offered the frog a confused look. "Whatever do you mean?" she asked worriedly.

Raspy let out a rude belch, then said, "Well, you are not exactly a beautiful princess. Why, step forward and take a good long look at your reflection in the lake, my dear. Look into the lake and you will see the truth of who you are."

Just then Raspyputin flicked his long, spindly fingers above the clear, green waters, and secretly cast a spell which caused the lake waters to sizzle, ripple, and then return to normal.

Ellie stepped forward and peered down into the lake.

The moment Ellie looked down at her image reflecting back at her from the clear, green water, she couldn't see any of the happy, good parts of her. The parts that made her shine like a bright light were suddenly very dim.

Instead what she saw peering back at her was
only the ugly side of her. "I'm so ugly!" Princess
Ellie gasped, fearfully. "What am I?"

Raspy let out a ribbit and said, "You, my dear, are
an Aye-aye!"

Staring at the frog in total confusion, Ellie asked,

"What is an Aye-aye?"

15

Raspy held up one spindly finger and said, "Shh! Listen!"

As if to emphasize his point, there came a shrill cry from the nearby trees, "Aye-aye! Aye-Aye! Aye-aye!"

Ellie peered up to the leafy branches of a tall oak tree, and there she spotted a small, furry, big-eared, bug-eyed creature staring down at her.

Raspy said, "That, my dear, is an Aye-aye. It is an evil animal. It hates everyone. It is so ugly that people detest it. They could never love it. They just pretend to love it."

In great distress, Ellie cried, "Why has no one ever told me? They told me I was a royal Princess of the Misty Forest!"

Raspy patiently explained to her, "They didn't want to offend you. Everyone knows–the King, the Queen, and all of your friends–that you are an evil, detestable creature. Isn't it nice of them not to make you feel bad?"

Raspy offered her a sad frown and said, "Why do you not remember all those awful things you've done in the past? Just the other day you upset your baby brother. Do you remember when he cried and wanted his Teddy, and instead of being kind and helping, you dropped Teddy into the garden? Mummy was very cross with you, but instead of saying you were sorry, you stamped your foot and marched out of the room."

Raspy continued, "Everyone can see how bad you are and, of course, no one really likes you. No one really cares about you."

Princess Ellie got more and more upset. "I don't think anyone loves me," she said.

"Yes, indeed!" Raspy readily agreed with her. "That must be true.

It's okay though. I can help you. If by chance you bump
into someone on your travels, you can pretend that there
is nothing wrong with you. Act totally normal. Maybe they
will love something you could create? Perhaps show them
how smart you are? Make them think you are really fun? It
doesn't really matter how, just do whatever you can to hide
your ugliness."

Raspy belched with delight. "Oh," he said, "there is one other thing. Have you ever met a Paladin? He's a Knight errant, a black Knight, who devours ugly Aye-aye's like you! If you ever see him, run for your life! He rides his horse through the wilds of the forest, hunting for prey to devour! You must be careful in case he comes your way!"

Ellie quietly, forlornly muttered, "Thank you for your advice."

Princess Ellie walked away from
the frog, solemnly and sadly. Raspy
offered her one last wicked scowl
that Ellie did not see as she left the
forest behind that day.

Many years went by, and Princess Ellie grew up
seeing only the evil inside her. When she met
others she would act as if nothing was wrong,
hiding the goodness inside of her in case
someone might see her evilness.

Sometimes others would wonder why the Princess seemed sad beneath her smile. She rejected love and affection from friends and family. She lost her glow. She felt hollow and empty inside. Every morning, she would peer into her mirror and she would see Aye-aye peering back at her. Slowly, others started to treat her like an Aye-aye. The life and love within her slowly ebbed away, and every year that went by, her ugliness got worse and worse until eventually she was nothing more than a bitter, twisted Aye-aye.

One day she was drinking from the lake, when she felt a warm breeze flowing down from the rustling leaves of the trees overhead. She looked up to see a butterfly glowing on a leaf, its yellow colour shining beautifully. Ellie watched the butterfly glide down from its leafy perch and drift away through the forest.

She decided to follow it. She saw another and another, dropping down from the branches above like a scattering of autumn leaves. Eventually, she came to a clearing in the forest where millions of butterflies filled the air.

They flew together to form an
image, and then in seconds they
scattered, leaving behind a cloud
of sparkling dust, and there
before Ellie stood a tall Knight
dressed in shimmering armour.

"The Paladin!" Ellie gasped in terror. "He has come
for me just like the frog warned me he would!"

Ellie tried to hide behind a tree, but the Paladin
simply stared at her curiously, wondering why the
young princess was trying to conceal herself.

Ellie cried, "Make it quick!"

"Make what quick?" the Paladin asked her, so majestic and powerful yet with a look of love upon his face, his long, silver hair curling past his broad shoulders.

Ellie said, "If you've come to devour me, do so quickly! I am an Aye-aye! I'm not very tasty. And if you eat me, you might become poisoned by the evil inside of me. Honestly, eating me would be a very bad idea."

The Paladin grinned in amusement. He asked, "Who told you, you are an Aye-aye? Most I have met are small, furry creatures, with big eyes, wide ears, and a long, skinny tail."

Ellie stepped out from behind the tree. "Look at me," she exclaimed in frustration, wondering if this Paladin was intelligent enough to see her for who she truly was. "I am an evil Aye-aye!"

The Paladin nodded knowingly, then said, "You have become an Aye-aye but that is not who you truly are. Do you know who I am?"

"You," Ellie said, "are the Paladin, the Black Knight, the rider who stalks through the forest delivering death to those you hunt!"

"Look again," the Paladin said, holding his hand out to her and producing a large globe of spinning light. "What do you see?"

Ellie looked at the golden globe of light held in the palm of the Paladin's hand, and at once images appeared there and she saw her loving mother who had raised her, a tear in her eye as she tightly embraced her.

Shocked by this scene, Ellie rubbed her eyes, and this time she saw the image of her friends appearing before her, warm smiles upon their faces. Ellie rubbed her eyes once more in disbelief, and when she opened her eyes this time there was nothing there.

The globe was gone, the Paladin who held it gone, too. She moved forward to where the Paladin had been standing, stepping into a beam of light that shone down through the leafy branches of the trees. The brilliant light surrounded her and embraced her. Ellie felt warm, peaceful, and safe, like she had felt when she was a baby in her father's arms. For the first time in years, her fear and guilt and shame were swept away.

A voice came from the rays:

"No more, little Aye-aye, no more.

No more will you live this lie."

The voice added, "You are not what you think
yourself to be. I am reclaiming you as one of
mine. Listen, my most beloved child, you are
the Princess of the Forest. The forest needs you.
Your friends need you. Your family needs you.
And I need you! I am going to make you the
most beautiful Princess once more. I am going to
take the Aye-aye away from you, if only you will
let me. Will you give me all your pain? All your
fears? Will you give to me your trust? I will carry
the Aye-aye far away, so it will never return,
but you must believe, for nothing can bring him
back, only in your mind will he live."

At once, a thousand butterflies fluttered around her, and shadows of darkness were carried off by the colourful, little wind-dancing butterflies. The voice said, "Open your heart and allow my love to soak into your heart like a soft rain pouring down from above. Allow my love to be your source to nourish the forest and all those you love. Endless rivers will run inside you. You are the source for the forest and for all those that come into contact with you. For you are the Princess of the Forest, the very essence that everything depends on because you have me inside you. I promise I will never leave you, and you will be forever protected under my wings.

"Remember one thing my beautiful Princess," the voice added, "there are many frogs around who would make you believe you are not what you are, but all tell lies far more than you can imagine. Remember I am always with you. Just close your eyes and I'll be there."

The Princess willingly opened her heart and welcomed the rain of butterflies pouring deep down into her being. After the tiny butterflies had passed through her, she felt strong and courageous, and the memories of the evil Aye-aye faded as the power of the love inside of her grew stronger. She lived for many years as the Princess of the Forest.

Everyone she met saw her glow and it brought so much healing to those that needed it. The forest flourished, brilliant shimmering colours returned, and her warmth and love was passed to all she met.

I share this tale to you and the girls beyond my realm of my journey as Princess Ellie. Many years have passed since I first met the kind Paladin. I tell you truly, you are a princess too, and a Paladin is heading your way. Do not run away but be courageous and open your heart to the gift that he offers. Don't be deceived by any evil frogs, for soon the Paladin will be with you. He is closer than you may realize, drawing near to you. May your forest grow in the majestic love all the days that you reign.

The End

Printed in the United States
By Bookmasters